Here's what some young mystery readers are saying about *Chase Under Pressure*:

"Grabs hold of you and doesn't let go."
—**Casey Fienberg**

"Just when you think you have everything figured out, think again."
—**Read Davis**

"Kept me guessing and on the edge of my seat."
—**Alexis Fringer**

"This book will go down in history!"
—**Max Thibert**

D1025585

Other Books by Steve Reifman

The Chase Manning Mystery Series
Chase Against Time (Chase Manning Mystery #1)
Chase for Home (Chase Manning Mystery #2)

Resource Books for Teachers and Parents
Changing Kids' Lives One Quote at a Time
2-Minute Biographies for Kids
22 Habits that Empower Students
Rock It!: Transform Classroom Learning with Movement, Songs, and Stories
Eight Essentials for Empowered Teaching and Learning, K-8
The First 10 Minutes: A Classroom Morning Routine that Reaches and Teaches the Whole Child
The First Month of School: Start Your School Year with 4 Priorities in Mind
Build a Partnership with Parents
Math Problem Solving Menus
The Ultimate Mystery Writing Guide for Kids

CHASE

Under Pressure

CHASE
Under Pressure

Chase Manning Mystery #3

STEVE REIFMAN

ISBN: 1508412448
ISBN 13: 9781508412441

To Mom, Dad, Lynn,
Jeff, Sylvia, Alan, Ari, and Jordy.

To all the family, friends, teachers,
and students whose support, expertise, and encour-
agement made this book possible.

Table of Contents

ACKNOWLEDGMENTS

I would like to acknowledge the wonderful work done by the entire CreateSpace team. You are all true professionals. It has been a genuine pleasure working with you.

I would also like to thank Amy Betz for her fantastic editing and Lorie DeWorken for her awesome cover design.

Tuesday, June 8th

CHAPTER 1

8:30 a.m.

"**A**ll right, everyone, time's up. Please put your pencils down and bring me your papers."

Nobody stopped.

The five of us who'd arrived at the small room behind the school auditorium an hour early today to take this science test knew what was at stake. We didn't want to hand in our work until we had double-checked every answer.

School Librarian Stanley Nelson tried again. "Boys and girls, we really must wrap things up now. We're finishing a few minutes later than I thought, and it's time to head back to your class. Please, I need your tests right away."

I walked up to Mr. Nelson's desk and turned in my test first.

"Thanks, Chase," he said, checking to see if my name was at the top of the paper. "Good luck today."

1

After I'd found the cello to save my school's music program just over two months ago and located the lucky batting glove that led to the baseball team's league championship last month, I couldn't wait for Apple Valley Elementary's next important event—this afternoon's big hamster race.

Students from eighteen schools would be there at 3:30 p.m. to see whose tiny creature would find the fastest path from the beginning of its maze to the tasty cheese at the end. The one that navigated the course the quickest would be declared the state's "Most A-Maze-ing Hamster."

Plus, the winning school would receive a $10,000 prize to buy new science equipment, and everyone on the winning team would earn free tuition for four weeks at a high-tech, sleep-away science camp this summer. Hopes were high at Apple Valley for our school's speedy little hamster, Dash.

I took my time packing up my stuff because I wanted to see everyone else finish. Jessica Kingman was the next person to bring Mr. Nelson her paper. With a smile of total confidence, she turned and shot me a look as she dropped her test on his desk. She had been trying to outshine me ever since she arrived at Apple Valley a couple months ago, and it still hadn't happened. She obviously thought her test score would be higher than mine and that today was finally going to be her day in the sun.

Jenny Gordon, my long-time neighbor and friend, and Lori Young arrived at Mr. Nelson's desk together a moment later. Jenny told me yesterday that she and Lori were especially excited about today's hamster competition because they both missed out on their gardening club's tomato showing a few weeks ago with terrible fevers.

Dave Morrison was the last to finish the test. Unlike Jessica and the other girls, Dave didn't appear confident. In fact, he looked downright gloomy as he handed in his paper with his initials "DM" written in the space where he was supposed to put his name. Nobody knew why, but Dave had done this for years. It had become his trademark.

Before the five of us left the testing room, Lori said, "Mr. Nelson, do we really need to take a test to pick the four people who can go downtown for today's race and try to win first prize?"

"I'm afraid so," the librarian replied.

"Even though there are only five of us trying out for the team?"

"I wish all five of you could enjoy this experience, but I'm afraid this is how it has to be."

3

"It doesn't seem fair," Lori lamented.

"I know," Mr. Nelson said. "I was as surprised as anybody when things changed. As you know, last week the rules said that each school could send five students to the race. I was happy that all of you could go because I know how hard you have worked over the past few weeks to get Dash ready for the contest. I'm sorry that the person with the lowest score won't be able to travel to today's hamster race with the team and have a chance to win the free spot at science camp."

"And why did the committee change the rules again?" Lori wondered.

"I don't know. They called out of the blue to tell us that now only four kids could represent our school."

"But why a test, Mr. Nelson? Couldn't we have flipped a coin or drawn straws to pick our team?" Lori asked.

"That's what I suggested, but your father thought that giving a test was the fairest thing to do. That way, the people who studied the hardest and wanted to be on the travel team the most would have the best chance to make it."

Even though Mr. Nelson was technically the leader of the science club and Lori's father was there to help, Mr. Young took over whenever he could. As a scientist himself and well-known animal rights activist, he wanted to be in charge. After what had happened recently with Alice Simmons and her

Gardening Angels, however, Principal Patty Fletcher decided that parents could no longer lead school clubs. So, she'd put Mr. Nelson in charge and made Mr. Young his assistant.

The librarian hadn't volunteered for this job. Although he loved science and animals, he didn't like competition. Ms. Fletcher had asked him to lead the club because she needed someone who didn't have a class of his own and had some free time during the day to take care of Dash and organize the hamster's supplies. That's what she'd told him at least.

"Anyway, kids, it's time for you to hustle back to class. Good luck, and I'll let you know as soon I'm done scoring the tests."

"Thanks, Mr. Nelson," Lori said. "I want to wish everybody luck also. We all deserve to be on this team, and we all have a good chance to make it."

"That's very nice of you to say, Lori."

As we left the testing room, I didn't know which four kids would get to be on the travel team for today's event. But there was one thing I did know.

Whoever didn't make it was going to be really mad.

8:43 a.m.

CHAPTER 2

8:44 a.m.

When Dave and I reached the auditorium door, we could hear Principal Fletcher talking to Lori's father down the hall.

"Good morning, Mark. How are you doing today?" asked Ms. Fletcher.

"I'm good, Patty. I just dropped Vicky off on the kindergarten playground, and I was hoping to catch Lori on her way back to class after her science test."

Mark Young was an important parent at Apple Valley. As the person who took over for Alice Simmons as head of the school's hiring committee after her daughter Amy was expelled, he was the one most responsible for giving Ms. Fletcher her dream job.

"How do you think Lori did?" she asked.

"I'm sure she did great," he responded. "Lori has always been a strong science student. That's why I decided not to draw straws and to give everyone the test this morning instead. I figured it would help her chances of being one of the four kids who represent our school today."

"Really? What did Stanley think of that idea?"

"I didn't ask him."

As Ms. Fletcher was about to respond, Lori Young emerged.

"Hi, Dad. Hi, Ms. Fletcher."

"Hi, sweetheart. How was the test?"

"It was fine, Dad. I think I did well."

"I'm sure you did," he said.

"I really hope I get to go to the race today. That science camp sounds cool!"

"You'll make the travel team, sweetheart," her father said reassuringly. "Science has always been your best subject."

Just then, Dave and I approached. The principal saw us and gave me a look. She was apparently still upset with me for something that happened the day I found my missing batting glove. I ended up getting the key to the gardening shed from my teacher, Mrs. Kennedy, after Ms. Fletcher had refused to give it to me. Even though I did nothing wrong in getting the key that way, Ms. Fletcher felt it was a disrespectful thing to do. She had made that clear to me several times since it happened.

While still talking with Lori and her father, Ms. Fletcher shot me another look and said, "Lori, I wish you the best of luck on the test. You're an excellent student, and you'd make a fine representative of the science team." With that, she turned around and walked with Mr. Young down the hall in the other direction.

I wasn't sure what that second look was all about and started walking with Dave back to our room. As of a couple weeks ago, the two of us were classmates. Dave's former teacher, Mrs. O'Connor, was worried that another student, Brock Fuller, was being a bad influence on him and wanted the two boys separated. So, she arranged to have Dave moved to Mrs. Kennedy's class.

As I was about to ask Dave how the test went, we noticed someone coming towards us.

It was Brock Fuller.

"Hey, Fan. Hey, Shovel, what's going on?" Brock still referred to me as "The Fan" because before using my grandpa's batting glove, I wasn't much of a hitter and seemed to do nothing except create a nice breeze with my swing for everyone in the immediate area. Brock called Dave "The Shovel" because of his *I Dig Gardening* T-shirt.

"Uh, hi, Brock," I said, hoping to keep this conversation short so we could head back to class.

"Where are you dudes coming from?" Brock asked.

"The auditorium. We had to take a science test at 7:30 to see which four people from the team can go to the hamster race today," I said.

"Wait a minute. Let me get this straight. You two dudes came to school early to take a *test*?"

"Yeah."

"I have just one thing to say to that."

"What?"

"Later."

After Brock walked away, I wanted to find out how things went for Dave on the test.

"I really studied hard for it," Dave said.

I wasn't sure if I was hearing correctly. Dave wasn't the most serious student in the world, and as Apple Valley's only true bully, he was known for spending his time in the principal's office, not getting ready for tests. In fact, I couldn't ever remember a time when Dave actually studied or cared about doing well in school.

"Yeah," Dave continued, "I really want to be on the travel team. So, I studied more than I ever have in my life. Since we found out we'd have to take this test, I have studied for it every morning and every night."

"That's awesome," I replied. "I hope your hard work pays off."

Up ahead in the hallway, Lori was talking with Jenny and Jessica. Fortunately, their voices were loud.

"Lori, what you said before we left the testing room was really nice," Jenny said.

"What are you talking about?" Lori asked.

"You said that you think we all deserve to be on the team and that we all have a good chance of making it."

"Oh, that. Forget about what I said in there. Dave Morrison has no chance of making this team."

"Huh?" asked a confused Jenny.

"Look, ladies," Lori said. "We've got it made. We're all going to make the team, and we're all going to camp together this summer—one way or another. It's that simple."

"How can you be so sure?" Jenny said.

"There are four spots on the travel team. Even if Chase gets one of them, that means Dave has to get a higher score on the test than one of us. That's not going to happen. He is simply no competition for us. We've got this thing in the bag."

Jenny appeared a bit uncomfortable with this kind of talk and tried to change the subject.

"But, Lori, I thought you were excited about the other camp we signed up for before we found out about the science camp."

"I was," Lori replied, "but the most important thing is that the three of us are going to be together."

"Yeah," Jessica added, "as long as we're together. All together."

"Even though the science camp doesn't have a swimming pool or the archery and ceramics activities you were looking forward to doing?" Jenny asked.

"Well, I will miss those things," Lori admitted. "But have you seen the brochure for the science camp? It has these cool, remote control cars, huge telescopes, and even a CSI crime lab!"

"Chase will like that," Jenny said.

Jessica groaned.

Jenny continued, "And you would be just as happy there as you'd be at the other camp?"

"I'll be happy as long as we're together," Lori stated once again.

"Yeah, as long as we're together," Jessica repeated. "You two are my best friends, and spending the summer together will be great, no matter where we go. And girls, can I tell you a little secret? I feel so good about our chances of making the team and winning the hamster race, I've even started buying new clothes! Lots of new clothes."

"Oh, that's nice!" Jenny said. "Admit it, though, Jess, being together for the summer isn't all you want, is it?"

"What do you mean?"

"You want to beat Chase on the test," Jenny teased.

"Well, maybe a little," Jessica admitted.

"Or maybe a lot."

"OK, maybe a lot."

8:54 a.m.

CHAPTER 3

8:55 a.m.

Back in Mrs. Kennedy's room, the five of us had settled in with our classmates and had begun working on today's math problem-solving activity. Given six toothpicks, each of us had to form as many triangles as possible, making sure that the toothpicks touched end-to-end. I usually loved challenges like these, but I had to admit, my mind was elsewhere. I was desperate to know which four people were going to make the travel team.

Suddenly, a figure appeared at our door.

It was Mr. Nelson.

"Mrs. Kennedy, I'm sorry to interrupt your students' learning, but may I sit in the back of the room for a little while? I need a place to score the science tests."

"Sure, but why can't you use the library?"

"Mr. Young was in there making a phone call, and he told me to leave."

"He told the *librarian* to leave the library?"

"Yes."

My teacher made a face and pointed to an open table. Mr. Nelson grabbed a seat and started grading the tests quietly. I was sitting a short distance away. I tried not to keep looking over at him, but it was hard. I was searching for even the smallest sign of whose test he was scoring and how it was going. Luckily, after finishing the second test, he became pretty chatty.

"Two down, three to go," Stanley Nelson mumbled to himself.

He then moved on to the third test. "Yes…yes…yes. Let's see. That's a score of 95%. Great job. I kind of expected that."

Please let that be mine. Please let that be mine, I thought.

After scoring the fourth test, Nelson uttered, "Well, she's always been such a good science student. That's no shock."

That must be Lori's, I figured. *Everyone knows science is her best subject.*

As the librarian began scoring the final test, he seemed confused. The more answers he read, the more puzzled he became. "Hmm, oh, my, wow, what a surprise."

Then he hesitated.

"I better double-check these to make sure I have every-thing right."

A short time later, he grabbed all the papers and hustled out the door.

I wonder what that was all about.

9:17 a.m.

CHAPTER 4

9:18 a.m.

Mrs. Kennedy was about to wrap up our toothpick activity when the intercom signal went off, indicating that an announcement from the office was on its way.

"Hello, boys and girls, this is Mr. Nelson. I'm here in the office with Mr. Young. I'm sorry to interrupt your learning, but I have some important news to share about today's hamster race. I'd like to read the names of the four people who will be representing Apple Valley at this afternoon's competition."

None of the kids in our class knew the team would be announced over the intercom, and we became very interested in hearing the names. Lori, Jenny, and Jessica crossed their fingers and looked at each other excitedly. Dave didn't look hopeful at all. I was feeling a few butterflies in my stomach.

Mr. Nelson continued. "Boys and girls, before I tell you the names, I just want to say how much I wish all five of the students who took the science test this morning could be part of today's event. Unfortunately, we're only allowed to take four. In my opinion, we—"

"Get on with it!" Mr. Young interrupted.

"Oh, yes, I'm sorry," Mr. Nelson said. "I will now read the four names in the order of the test scores, starting with the highest score. The first member of the team is a very nice young girl from Mrs. Kennedy's class. She's obviously a strong science student. Her name is Jenny Gordon."

As everyone in the room clapped for Jenny, Lori turned to Jessica and whispered, "That's one, Jess. You and I are next."

"The second member of the team is also from Mrs. Kennedy's class," Mr. Nelson said.

Jessica and Lori smiled at each other.

Mr. Nelson went on. "This student is also a very nice young person. He's been involved in quite a bit of excitement around school lately. His name is Chase Manning."

As the other kids cheered for me, I looked back at the girls. Lori didn't seem worried at this point, probably because there were still two more spots on the team. Jessica, however, was fuming.

Wow, she must have really wanted to get a higher score than me on the test, I thought.

"The next student, excuse me, the next team member—"

"I've had it! You're taking too long," Mr. Young interrupted, growing impatient and grabbing the microphone away from Mr. Nelson. "I'll say the rest of the names."

Poor Mr. Nelson. He was simply doing the job Ms. Fletcher asked him to do. I couldn't believe Mr. Young had the nerve to interfere like that. The librarian, however, wasn't the type to cause a scene, and he didn't put up a fight.

Immediately, Lori Young sat taller in her chair. A big smile appeared on her face. She was probably thinking how cool it would be to have her own father announce her name to the whole school.

"Boys and girls, hello, this is Mr. Young. The third member of the team is Jessica Kingman."

Some of the kids clapped for Jessica. She and Jenny looked confidently at Lori. They were all on the edge of their seats, expecting Lori's name to be announced as the last member of the team. That way, no matter what happened at the race this afternoon, the three girls would be going to camp together this summer.

"The fourth and final member of the team will be...what? What's this? This can't be right. Is this right?" he asked Mr. Nelson.

"It's right, Mr. Young."

"Are you sure?"

"Yes, sir. I checked each test myself, twice."

"Uh, I can't believe it," stammered Mr. Young.

All of a sudden, we heard a thud. Maybe Mr. Young fell off his chair.

Mr. Nelson grabbed the microphone and finished the announcement. "Boys and girls, the fourth and final member of the team is Dave Morrison."

Dave was beaming when he heard his name. I had never seen him look so proud.

The three girls were stunned.

9:28 a.m.

CHAPTER 5

9:29 a.m.

Our classroom was in shock after hearing that Dave Morrison, not Lori Young, would be the fourth member of the science team representing our school at this afternoon's big hamster race. The three girls couldn't believe that Dave got a higher score on the test than Lori, ending their chance to go to science camp together. Earlier, I heard them discussing their plans for the summer. Those plans were now in jeopardy.

Their reaction to the news was so strong that I wondered whether they heard the end of Mr. Nelson's announcement. He asked all five of the test takers to report upstairs to the library immediately with our backpacks for this morning's special exhibition. The team from Diamond Elementary, which had traveled to Apple Valley from across the state, was visiting nearby schools as part of a "Goodwill Tour" and was due to arrive in the next few minutes. During the exhibition Diamond Elementary's hamster was going to face Dash in a friendly warm-up for this afternoon's competition.

As eager as I was to see Diamond's hamster, I was far more interested in checking out the team's captain, Ricky Dempsey. Stories about Ricky and his outrageous personality had become legendary lately, and nobody was sure how many of them were actually true.

Lori was pouting with her arms folded across her chest and her lower lip almost touching her nose as she entered the library, well behind the rest of us.

"Mr. Nelson, why am I even here if I'm not part of the team?" she asked with fierce eyes.

"Well, since you can't travel with us later today, I thought it would be nice if you could at least join us for Diamond Elementary's visit this morning."

Lori didn't seem grateful for the opportunity.

We all walked through the main part of the library to a back section that had two rooms. The first one had recently become known as the Maze Room because that's where Mr. Nelson kept Dash and stored her food, practice mazes, and other equipment. The exhibition race was going to take place there.

My favorite piece of equipment was the special tracking device that monitored Dash's pulse rate. While she wore a tiny patch on her skin, the machine made a soft beeping noise as long as her pulse rate was in a healthy range. The tracking device was so powerful that as long as Dash was somewhere on campus, it would work.

Next door to the Maze Room was an area that one student nicknamed the Party Room because that's where the two teams would enjoy punch and cookies after the exhibition race. Interestingly, that person was Lori. Right now, she wasn't in the mood for any party.

We dropped off our backpacks in the far corner of the Maze Room, as we always did when we worked with Dash. Mr. Young and Ms. Fletcher were in the opposite corner talking. Eager to get a good view of the action, the four travel team members sat in the first row of chairs and waited for the Diamond Elementary team to arrive. Lori, still pouting, sat by herself in the third row.

After staring for a few minutes at the tables Mr. Nelson had set up for the two mazes, I noticed a commotion at the library door. Sure enough, Ricky Dempsey was ready to make his grand entrance. Diamond Elementary's leader and three other team members came in first, with the adult and one student standing off to the left and the other two kids standing to the right, forming a walkway for Ricky and the school's hamster, Diamond.

With his arms raised in a "V," Ricky swaggered inside, holding the hamster in his right hand.

"Have no fear, boys and girls, Ricky's here. That's right, one-of-a-kind Ricky Dempsey. The one you've heard so much about is here at…at…hey, where are we again?" Ricky asked, turning toward the team leader with his hand shielding his mouth.

"Apple Valley Elementary, Ricky," the man softly responded.

"Apple Valley Elementary!" Ricky proudly declared.

"Who does this guy think he is?" I whispered to Jenny.

"I don't know," she replied.

"Ricky's hamster is ready to rock and roll. That's right, rock and roll. Diamonds may be a girl's best friend, but this Diamond is every hamster's worst nightmare."

"This is a *goodwill* visit?" I whispered to Jenny.

"Yeah."

"I'm not feeling much goodwill."

"Neither am I," she replied.

"Ricky's hamster is undefeated, untested, and unchallenged," he bragged.

"I think all those stories we heard about this guy are true," I whispered.

"I think so, too," Jenny replied.

Eventually, the Diamond team sat down in the second row of chairs, and Ms. Fletcher walked to the front of the room to start the exhibition. Mr. Nelson and Mr. Young joined her.

"Good morning, everybody," Ms. Fletcher began. "I'm so happy to welcome you to this morning's special exhibition. It's nice to see all of you here today. It's extremely nice to see you, Dave Morrison. Congratulations on your high test score."

Dave smiled in a way that I had never seen before. He was bursting with pride after doing so well on this morning's test, and he especially seemed to like being recognized for something positive. Who knows? Maybe this could be a new beginning for him.

Then, Ms. Fletcher continued. "As I was saying, Dave, it's extremely nice to see you—somewhere other than my office. I mean, you have been spending almost as much time in there lately as I have," she said.

I couldn't believe what a cheap shot Ms. Fletcher had taken at Dave. As the principal, she should be supporting him, not spoiling such a special day with cruel and unfair comments.

A moment later, Ms. Fletcher asked Mr. Nelson to introduce the four members of the travel team.

"Hello, everyone, my name is Stanley Nelson, and I am the librarian here at Apple Valley. I'm so happy for the four students who will represent our school this afternoon. No matter who wins and who loses, I want all the children to have a positive experience. I—"

"I've had it! You're taking too long," Mr. Young interrupted, growing impatient and grabbing the microphone away from the librarian.

Mr. Nelson mumbled a few things under his breath about Mr. Young's rude behavior and went to sit down. The librarian found a chair next to Lori, who was still pouting, and he noticed the anguish on her face. He obviously felt bad for her and regretted that this competition had caused her such hard feelings.

Mr. Young went on to introduce the Apple Valley team. Next, Diamond Elementary's leader introduced his group. Both teams then walked to their tables to get into ready position.

The exhibition was about to begin.

9:47 a.m.

CHAPTER 6

9:48 a.m.

"**O**K, everybody, you know the rules," Mr. Young said as he was about to start the race. "We put the hamsters in the entrance on one side of the maze and the cheese at the exit on the other side. The hamster that goes through the maze the fastest and finds the cheese first is the winner."

Mr. Young was right. We did already know the rules. When he finished talking, we started encouraging our hamsters.

"Come on, Dash, you can do it," I said.

"It's time to rock and roll, Diamond! Rock and roll! You can do it, baby! Ricky knows you can do it. Ricky feels good to-day! Later this afternoon, you'll be sending Ricky to camp, send-ing Rick-y to camp!"

"Does this guy ever stop talking?" I whispered to Jenny.

"I don't know," she whispered back.

"Diamond is going to be flying today!" Ricky proclaimed. "That's a fact, Jack."

"Are you talking to me?" I asked Ricky.

"Huh?"

"You said *Jack*. I thought you called me Jack."

"No, Ricky didn't call you Jack."

"Well then, who's Jack?"

"Nobody, Jack is nobody," Ricky said, shaking his head at me. "Ricky is just using an expression."

"Oh."

Ricky went right back to his cheerleading. "You're the best, Diamond, the best. That's the truth, Ruth."

"Are you talking to me?" Jenny asked Ricky.

"Huh?"

"You said *Ruth*. I thought you called me Ruth."

"No, Ricky didn't call you Ruth."

"Well then, who's Ruth?"

"Nobody, Ruth is nobody," Ricky said, shaking his head at Jenny and growing exasperated. "Ricky is just using an expression. Ricky speaks the truth, that's all. Ricky speaks the truth."

"Oh."

Ricky couldn't understand why we didn't understand him.

I was beginning to enjoy watching Ricky get annoyed. I thought I'd ask him another question.

"Ricky, you named your hamster after your school?"

"Yeah," he said with disappointment.

I noticed Ricky's tone and said, "Did you want to name him something else?"

"Yeah."

"What?"

"*Ricky*, of course. What else?"

I decided that the time for fun and games was over. I turned my attention back to Dash.

Right before the race began, Ricky turned to me and asked one last question. "Hey, Jack, Ricky wants to know something. How long does it usually take your hamster to finish this maze?"

"About 17 or 18 seconds."

Ricky started laughing. He tried to hold it back, but he couldn't. "17 or 18 seconds, you say?"

"Yes, but her best is 16.7 seconds," Jenny said, standing up for her hamster.

"Ricky's hamster is usually around 14 or 15 seconds. Diamond's best time is a cool 13.9. Ricky wishes you all good luck. You're going to need it."

"OK, everybody, enough talking," Mr. Young said, taking control of the situation. "Let's get started. Hamsters, on your mark, get set, go!"

Both teams were screaming at the top of their lungs as the hamsters began their mazes. Diamond got off to a good start, but Dash was absolutely flying. In an instant, it was over. Dash had beaten Diamond with a stunning time of 12.1 seconds.

Ricky was speechless.

"Th-th-that's a really fast hamster you all have here. R-R-Ricky's never seen anything like it."

The color drained from his face.

Jenny, Jessica, Dave, and I smiled, complimented Dash, and put her in her tiny cage so she could rest. As our team was celebrating Dash's performance, Ricky simply fell back in his chair.

Dash had just rocked Ricky's world.

10:00 a.m.

CHAPTER 7

10:01 a.m.

The whole purpose of Diamond Elementary's visit to Apple Valley was for the kids on both teams to spend some time together and get to know one another before this afternoon's hamster competition.

That wasn't happening.

Instead of mingling at the party after the exhibition race, the two teams pretty much kept to themselves. Lori Young was off in one corner of the Party Room by herself, still sulking. Ricky Dempsey sat alone in another corner; he was taking Diamond's first loss hard. The other three members of Ricky's team were also upset, though none reacted quite the way he had. They were talking quietly by the refreshment table.

The only people who seemed to realize that this was a party were Jenny, Jessica, Dave, and me. We were laughing, high-fiving, and snapping up all the cookies in sight.

As Ms. Fletcher left the room to take care of some business and Mr. Nelson was chatting with Diamond's team leader, Mr. Young came over to our group and said, "Hey, guys, let's not get too excited. Yes, Dash was terrific this morning, but this is only a practice race. We haven't won anything yet."

He was right.

"I know you want to celebrate," he continued, "but those kids over there drove a long way to be here. Let's make them feel welcome and help them have some fun."

My teammates and I walked over to start a conversation with the members of the Diamond team. Within a few minutes the party was starting to look like a real party, and everyone, except Lori and Ricky, was having a good time. Mr. Nelson put on some music, and the mood became even more festive. After a while there wasn't a cookie to be found.

All of a sudden, I saw Ricky walk up to his team leader and whisper something in the man's ear. Shortly after that, the leader instructed the Diamond team members to gather their stuff and get ready to head back to the bus.

Mr. Young also saw what was happening and approached the Diamond leader. "Is everything all right?" he asked.

"Oh, yes, Mr. Young," he responded. "We need to head out a little early today."

"I thought you and your team were going to stay until 10:30?"

"Uh, yeah, we were, but..." the leader said, turning to look at Ricky. After Ricky glared back at him, the man continued. "Uh, we were, but the traffic was very heavy on the way here, and we wanted to leave a little early so we could get a head start to the next school on our schedule."

"We'll see you later today then."

"Uh, yeah, later today," he said hesitantly. "Thanks, Mr. Young."

The two team leaders asked everybody to shake hands and say their goodbyes. Hearing this direction, Ricky didn't waste any time. He came right up to me, shook my hand, and, while holding the handshake firmly, looked me straight in the eye. "Your hamster was good this morning," he said, "but let's see how she does this afternoon when it really matters. Let's see if she shows up later today the way she showed up this morning."

Ricky then broke the handshake and walked away.

Show up? What does that mean? It's probably another one of Ricky's expressions. Well, at least this time he didn't call me Jack.

Once the party ended, our team stuck around for a few minutes to clean up and put everything away. Jenny, Jessica, Dave, and I were talking about Dash's electrifying performance, and I had an idea.

"Hey, everybody," I said, "let's go congratulate Dash one more time before we go downstairs."

The other three smiled, and we walked into the Maze Room. When we got there, something didn't seem quite right. The tables and chairs that Mr. Nelson had set up were still there. So was the maze we had used in the exhibition. But when we looked for the hamster's little cage, we couldn't find it.

As we stared at one another in disbelief, we all realized the same thing.

Dash was gone.

10:15 a.m.

CHAPTER 8

10:16 a.m.

"**I** can't believe this!" exclaimed Mr. Nelson when we told him, Mr. Young, and Ms. Fletcher what we had discovered.

"This is terrible!" I said.

"This is awful!" Dave agreed.

"I hope she's OK!" Jenny added.

"She's not really gone, is she?" Jessica panicked.

Lori and her father said nothing.

"Could Dash have run out of the room?" the principal asked.

"No, Ms. Fletcher, we locked her in her little cage after the race so she could rest," I replied.

"And the cage is also gone?" she asked.

"Yes, someone stole the cage with Dash still inside of it," I concluded.

"What are we supposed to do now?" Jessica asked.

"We don't have a minute to waste," I said, turning toward the principal. "Ricky must have taken her when we weren't looking. I can see through the window that his bus is still downstairs, and we need to go talk to him right now!"

"How can you be so sure that Ricky did it?" the principal asked.

"You saw the look on his face when Dash beat Diamond. He was devastated."

"Is that the only reason you suspect Ricky?"

"No, I also saw him whisper something to his team leader during the party, and then a minute later, they left. It was almost as if Ricky told the leader that the team had to leave right away."

"I'm not sure about this, Chase," she said. "I don't think we should go around suspecting and accusing our school visitors. It just doesn't seem like you have that much evidence."

"Wait, there's more," I fired back, not really understanding why she was making this so hard for me. "Right before Ricky left, he told me he wasn't sure whether Dash would 'show up' later this afternoon. At first, I thought it was one of his expressions, but now I'm thinking he took her so she wouldn't actually show up at the race and beat his hamster again."

"Oh, I'm still not sure, Chase."

"Ms. Fletcher, the bus is going to leave any minute. We need to get down there right now. This is our only chance to catch Ricky before he goes!"

"I don't think that's such a good idea."

"Why not? Please, Ms. Fletcher, let me go down there. It will only take a minute," I pleaded. I was beginning to get antsy.

"I'm afraid I can't do that, Chase. You see, the bus is parked on the street. Technically, that area is outside of the school boundaries, and I can't let anyone out there without a signed permission slip, like when we go on field trips."

Was she kidding? I wasn't sure at this point whether she was simply following the rules or if there was something else going on here.

All of a sudden, a loud noise interrupted the conversation.

"Ms. Fletcher, that noise is the bus. The engine is starting, and they're going to leave now. I have to go down there."

"Chase, you heard what I said. For the last time, the answer is no."

"But—"

"Listen to her, son!" Mr. Young interrupted. "You may not go out there!"

I began to get even antsier, and to the surprise of everyone in the room, I took off and bolted downstairs.

The three girls looked at one another in disbelief.

Dave Morrison was proud of me.

Patty Fletcher was furious.

As I reached the front gate of the school, I took a look over my shoulder and noticed that everyone upstairs had moved to the window and could see all the action unfold before their very eyes.

"Yes!" I yelled to myself as I looked up the street and saw that the bus was still there.

I decided to make a run for it.

When I was only five feet away from the back of the bus, it began to pull away.

"Stop!" I screamed. "Stop the bus!"

But it didn't stop.

Sitting in the back of the bus and watching the whole thing was Ricky Dempsey. He gave me a big annoying smile and waved goodbye as the bus rumbled down the street.

Realizing that a golden opportunity had been lost by no more than a few seconds, I bent over, put my hands on my knees, and started huffing and puffing in frustration.

A minute later I looked up at the library window and saw Ms. Fletcher glaring down and shaking her finger at me. I felt a terrible knot in my stomach.

It was shaping up to be another one of those days.

10:27 a.m.

CHAPTER 9

10:28 a.m.

My teammates and I were dejected as we arrived back in class prior to the start of recess. I didn't even have a chance to sit down before Mrs. Kennedy called me up to her desk with the news. Ms. Fletcher wanted to see me upstairs in the library.

Now.

Dreading the conversation that was about to take place, I wondered why the two of us would be talking in the library and not in her office. With everything else that had already gone on today, though, I decided not to ask.

"Chase, come in," Ms. Fletcher said calmly when she saw me arrive.

Because another class was using the main part of the library, the principal and I found two chairs in the Maze Room.

"Do you know why I asked to speak with you?" Ms. Fletcher began.

"I think so."

"Then you know what you did was wrong?"

Before I could answer, something caught my attention, and I began to look around the room trying to figure out what it was.

"Chase, are you listening to me?"

"I'm sorry, Ms. Fletcher, did you hear that?"

"Hear what?"

"That sound."

"No, Chase, I didn't hear any sound. We're here to talk about you and how you—"

"Ms. Fletcher, I'm sorry to interrupt you, but don't you hear that sound? There's a beeping sound. It's coming from somewhere in this room."

"Chase, forget the beeping sound!" she snapped. "I'm trying to talk to you about something important."

Then it hit me.

"The pulse tracker!" I shouted. "The beeping sound is coming from the tracker! Ms. Fletcher, do you know what this means?"

"No," she responded, her frustration growing.

"The tracker only works when Dash is within the boundaries of the school. The beeping means Dash is still here! Ricky didn't take her. She's still here! She's still here!"

After explaining everything to her, I expected my principal to be as excited as I was.

She wasn't.

I also expected her to put aside our conversation about my behavior and start focusing on finding Dash.

She didn't.

Instead, all she wanted was to lecture me about the importance of respecting authority. All I wanted was to get out of that room and start investigating. Since the upper grade classes were outside at recess, I'd be able to talk to everyone.

"Ms. Fletcher, I'm sorry about what I did. You asked me not to go out to the bus, and I did. I didn't think I had any other choice. Ricky was leaving, I thought he took Dash, and I had to act fast. May I go now?"

"I'm not sure you understand my point."

"I do. Believe me, I do," I protested.

"I'm not sure about that. You keep looking around, and you seem to have something else on your mind. You seem preoccupied. I think I need to explain things to you one more time."

"I understand, Ms. Fletcher, but recess is going to be over soon, and I want to start investigating who might have taken Dash."

"I'm afraid I can't let you leave quite yet," she replied.

As the principal kept lecturing, I began to wonder if there was another reason she was keeping me there. Her talking seemed to go on forever. After a few more minutes, she checked her watch. She smiled and said, "Chase, I think you've learned your lesson. You may go now."

Relieved, I thanked Ms. Fletcher, got up from my chair, and bolted to the door.

Just then, the bell rang. Recess was over.

I was furious.

"Oh, there's one more thing," Ms. Fletcher added, as if taking away my entire recess wasn't enough. "Whatever you do, remember what I am about to tell you next."

I didn't say anything. I just turned and looked the principal right in the eye as she finished her statement.

"Don't ever disobey me again."

10:46 a.m.

CHAPTER 10

10:47 a.m.

Though I was incredibly upset with Ms. Fletcher for ruining my plan, I tried to stay calm.

"We have to tell everyone about this," I said. "The others need to know that Dash is still somewhere on campus."

After hesitating a moment, she agreed. She didn't seem happy about it. "Fine, you go round up the others while I call Mr. Young and Mr. Nelson."

I hustled outside and saw Jenny lining up after the bell. I yelled down and asked her to gather everyone and tell Mrs. Kennedy that the principal wanted us for a short meeting. A few minutes later the two men arrived, followed shortly thereafter by Dave, Jenny, Jessica, and Lori.

What is she doing here? I wondered to myself when I saw Lori enter with the others. *I thought this meeting was for travel team members only. Well, I guess it couldn't hurt if she stayed.*

With everyone huddled together, Ms. Fletcher shared the news about Dash.

"That's great!" Jenny said. "We have to find her. What do we do now? What's our first step?"

Immediately, all the other kids and adults looked at me, assuming I would know how to proceed.

"Well," I said, flattered by everyone's confidence in me, "we should probably search this room first before looking anywhere else on campus."

"That makes sense to me," nodded Ms. Fletcher. "Go ahead, everybody, let's see what we can find in here."

As the three adults huddled together, my classmates and I spread out and searched every inch of the Maze Room.

"Wait! I found something!" Lori exclaimed.

Everyone rushed over to her.

"What is it?" Jessica asked.

"It's a crumpled up piece of paper. I think it's a note."

"Read it to us, sweetheart," her father instructed.

"It says: 'Ha, ha, ha, looking for Dash? Don't waste your time. You'll never find her. By the way, I just dig hamsters. Signed, DM.' "

All eyes instantly turned towards Dave. Because of his gardening T-shirt and because he always signed his papers with his initials, he quickly became the number one suspect.

"Dave Morrison, how could you do such a thing?" the principal snapped.

"But I didn't do it!" he protested.

"Dave?"

"I swear, I didn't steal the hamster!"

"But, Dave, how am I supposed to believe you? Your initials are right there on the note."

"Why would I sign a note like that? You have to believe me. I made the team this time. I couldn't be on the baseball team. I couldn't be in the orchestra. But I *made* the science team. I studied hard for the test, and I made the team. It doesn't make sense. Why would I take Dash when I finally made the team?"

I had never seen Dave so emotional. Whenever he was caught misbehaving, which, I had to admit, happened a lot in the short time Ms. Fletcher had been principal, he usually accepted his punishment quietly.

That wasn't happening today.

He was putting up quite a fight. Even though he kept denying it, Ms. Fletcher was not ready to cut him any slack or give him the benefit of any doubt.

"Young man, I think we need to discuss this matter privately," she said. "We're going to my office."

While Ms. Fletcher was scolding Dave by the door, the three girls began whispering to one another off to the side of the room. I wanted to hear what they were saying, but I didn't want them to know I was listening. So, I knelt to the ground and pretended to tie my shoelaces.

"Do you realize what this means, ladies?" Lori asked with a big smile forming on her face.

"No, what does it mean?" Jessica responded.

"Dave is going to get kicked off the science team because he took Dash, right?" Lori explained.

"Yeah, I guess so," Jessica said.

"Well, if we find her, then Daddy, I mean, Mr. Nelson and my father, will put me on the team to take his place. And no matter what happens in the race this afternoon, our plans for the summer will be back on again. If we win, we'll be going to science camp together, and if we lose, we'll be going to the other camp."

"Whoa, you may be right," Jessica said.

"Of course I am," Lori replied. "Cheer up, ladies. This is going to be a beautiful afternoon."

"Chase," Ms. Fletcher announced, "you and the girls go back to class. I need to take Dave down to the office."

"Ms. Fletcher," I replied, "we were all supposed to meet up here at 2:45 to get ready for today's contest. Do you still want us here, even though we haven't found Dash?"

"Yes," the principal responded without hesitation.

Dave continued protesting as Ms. Fletcher escorted him out of the library.

"Come with me, Dave. Now."

"But I'm telling the truth! It wasn't me! It wasn't me!"

As the girls headed downstairs, I stood alone, thinking. Ms. Fletcher may have been sure that Dave took Dash. So may have the others. But I wasn't convinced.

Something didn't seem right.

11:02 a.m.

CHAPTER 11

11:03 a.m.

"**W**e have to figure out who really took Dash," I said to Jenny as we returned to class.

"What are you talking about? I think it's pretty obvious this time. Dave did it."

"I don't think so," I replied. "I know his initials were found on the note, but did you see how he reacted?"

"Yeah, he said he didn't do it. What would you expect him to say?"

"It wasn't only what he said. It was how he said it. He was angry. Usually, when he gets in trouble, he accepts his punishment quietly. He didn't do that this time. He was really mad."

"And you think he's innocent?" Jenny asked.

"Yes."

"Why?"

"First of all, you heard what he said a minute ago. He's right. Why would he do it? You saw him this morning when his name was announced on the intercom. It was probably the proudest moment of his life."

"And you think somebody else took Dash?"

"Yes."

"Why?"

"The note. Why would he write a note and put his initials on it? Dave is smarter than that. You think he would ruin his chance to do something cool the first time he's allowed on a team? Something doesn't add up here. Somebody must have stolen Dash and wanted to make it look like Dave did it."

"Frame Dave? You really think that someone is framing Dave?"

"Yes."

"Come on, Chase, tell me who—"

"Hang on a minute. I need to do something."

A second later, I was out of my chair and on my way to see Mrs. Kennedy.

"Boy, he can be exasperating," Jenny said to herself, probably not realizing that I could still hear her.

"Mrs. Kennedy, you heard about Dash, didn't you?" I asked.

"Unfortunately, I did," she said, shaking her head. "It's such a shame that weird boy from Diamond Elementary took her."

"No, Mrs. Kennedy, she's still here. We just found out that Ricky didn't take her. Dash is still somewhere on campus. The thing is, everyone thinks Dave did it, but I don't think that's right. I think he's being framed, and I need to go to the office to talk to Ms. Fletcher. May I go while the others are at PE?"

"Well, Chase, that story seems a bit hard to believe, but I have learned from you recently that just because something seems hard to believe, it doesn't mean it's not true. Sure, go ahead. Try not to take too long, though."

"Thanks, Mrs. Kennedy. I'll go as fast as I can."

I was so excited that my teacher gave me permission to go to the office, I reached out and gave her a nice fist bump.

"What the heck?" I said to myself.

I made my way down the hall to the office. When I arrived, I passed the baseball trophy in the entryway. Watching it shine in the light brought back some wonderful memories, but I didn't have time to think about them now. I noticed through the blinds that Mr. Young was with Ms. Fletcher in her office. From where I was standing, I could see their faces, but they couldn't see mine. Fortunately, I was able to hear their conversation.

"I want you to throw the book at him this time!" Mr. Young demanded.

"I hear what you're saying, and I understand your frustration," the principal replied. "I mean, after all the time and hard work you and your team have put into this race, for Dave to steal Dash, he needs to pay."

"Oh, yes," Mr. Young added, "he needs to pay dearly, especially after what happened last time."

"You're obviously referring to the incident involving Dave and your daughter that occurred earlier this year."

"You bet I am! Lori was lucky to come away from that episode unharmed, and you know I thought your punishment for Dave was far too light."

"Yes, you have made that clear numerous times."

"I am determined not to let that happen again. Oh, and one more thing."

"What's that?"

"If we find Dash," Mr. Young continued, "I want Dave off the science team, and I want the alternate to replace him."

Dave was sitting on the chair right outside the principal's office. He'd already spotted me. I approached him cautiously because Ms. Fletcher had a clear view of him. When I was still a few feet away, Dave covered his mouth with his hands and whispered to me, "I didn't do it. I swear."

I gave him a wink and knocked on Ms. Fletcher's door.

"Chase, what can I do for you?" she asked.

"May I speak to you two for a minute, please?"

"Yes," they answered.

"Should we bring in Mr. Nelson, too? After all, he is the leader of the science club, and that's what I wanted to talk to you about."

"Fine," Ms. Fletcher said. She picked up the phone and began dialing the librarian's extension.

"That's not necessary," Mr. Young said, grabbing the phone and placing it back down. "He doesn't need to be here. Whatever you have to say, just say it to us."

"OK," I began, "I don't think Dave took Dash. I know we found the note, but I think someone else wrote it and is trying to frame him."

Ms. Fletcher and Mr. Young looked at each other skeptically. I went on to explain my reasoning.

After hearing what I had to say, Ms. Fletcher didn't say a word. Mr. Young, on the other hand, was ready with a response.

"You go ahead and try to prove your case. If you do, and if you find Dash, we'll keep Dave on the team."

"You will?"

"Yes, but you'll need to do all this by the time we meet back in the Maze Room at 2:45."

"But that's only three hours from now!"

"Well then, you better get cracking," Mr. Young said, slamming the door in my face.

Dave and I exchanged confused looks.

"I don't get it," I shared. "The school is going to get $10,000 for science equipment if we win. That's a ton of money. We'll get to go to an awesome camp, and Apple Valley will get a lot of attention around the state."

"What's your point?" Dave asked.

"My point is that these two," I said, gesturing toward the principal's office, "should be helping me find Dash, but they're not. They should be making things easier for me, but they're making everything harder. I don't get it."

Just then, the door to the principal's office opened.

"Chase, you need to leave now," Ms. Fletcher said.

"But I only need to talk to Dave for a minute."

"Do I have to remind you, Chase, about our conversation earlier about respecting authority?"

"No, ma'am, I'll leave right now."

"Good."

As I walked back through the entryway, I knew I had to find a way to talk with Dave alone without upsetting Ms. Fletcher. I needed to get information that would help clear his name and keep him on the team.

Outside the office door, I saw Mr. Nelson coming down the hallway. I told the librarian about the meeting I'd had with Mr. Young and Ms. Fletcher about the science team.

"Why wasn't I invited to the meeting?"

"The principal was about to call you, but Mr. Young said you didn't need to be there."

"Why, the nerve of that guy!" Mr. Nelson said, walking away in a huff.

Before returning to class, I stayed outside the office for a minute. I closed my eyes, dropped my chin to my chest, and tried to figure out a way to speak with Dave privately.

Then, out of nowhere, it hit me!

I knew exactly what I was going to do.

Only one question remained.

Would I be able to pull it off?

11:25 a.m.

CHAPTER 12

11:26 a.m.

I took a few deep breaths and bounced from side to side to get myself ready to put my plan into action. I had never done anything like this before and wasn't sure how it was going to turn out. After reviewing all the details one last time in my head, I opened the office door and headed right back inside.

While walking toward Dave, I turned my head and looked into the principal's office.

"Hi, Ms. Fletcher, I'm just—"

And then it happened.

I rammed right into Dave, knocking him out of his chair and sending both of us to the hard tile floor.

Down on the ground, Dave growled in pain. "Ow, what was that for?"

"Grab your nose," I immediately whispered back to him.

"What? Why do you want—"

"Shh, just grab your nose!" I instructed.

Dave grabbed his nose.

I reached for my wrist.

"Oh, I am such a klutz!" I yelled.

We were writhing in pain on the floor.

"Ms. Fletcher!" I wailed. "We're hurt! Dave injured his nose, and I banged my wrist. Can we please go to the nurse's office to get some ice?"

"What? How did this...oh, fine, hurry up, go ahead," she said.

Though my wrist really did hurt, I was beaming on the inside. Now, the two of us would be free to talk privately, away from the watchful eye of Patty Fletcher.

"Hello, boys, what do we have here?" Nurse Carlton said as we entered her office.

"Hi, Mrs. Carlton, we're going to need some ice. Would you mind going to the cafeteria to get some for my wrist and Dave's nose?" I asked, beginning part two of my plan.

"I should have enough ice in here for both of you," she replied.

"Oh," I said, caught off guard a bit. "Actually, Dave took a pretty nasty fall. I think he also hurt his knees and elbows."

"My goodness! For all those injuries, I will need to go to the cafeteria. Hold on. I'll be back as soon as I can."

"No rush."

Once the nurse left the room, I sprang into action.

"Dave, we need to talk."

"Chase, I didn't do this. You have to believe me."

"I do believe you, Dave, but I may be the only one around here who does."

Dave wasn't used to having anybody stick up for him. He smiled.

"I'll help prove you didn't do it," I said, "but, no offense, with your reputation it's not going to be easy."

Dave sat there quietly in agreement. He knew I was right.

"We need to do two things," I told him. "We have to find Dash, and we have to find out who took her."

Dave's smile grew even larger.

"Why are you so happy?" I asked.

"It's just that I really like having you on my side for a change. How are we going to do these two things?"

"I'm not sure yet," I replied. "I need to go back to class to talk to Jenny. You're going to have to stay here. Before I go, is there anything you can say that will help me?"

"Like what?"

"Like, where were you at the end of the party when Dash was taken?"

"I was drinking punch and standing around with everyone else."

"Did you leave at all to go into the Maze Room? Even for a minute?"

"Just once."

Oh, no, I thought to myself.

"No, I didn't do anything wrong. I swear," Dave said, seeing the worried look on my face. "I only went to grab my backpack. I promise."

"That's it?"

"That's it."

"Did you see anyone in there?"

"I saw Jenny, Lori, and Jessica, but they left as soon as I got there."

"Then?"

"Then Mr. Young and Mr. Nelson came in, and Mr. Young barked at me to get back to the party."

"And you didn't write that note with your initials on it?"

"Come on, give me a break. I know I'm no genius, but I'm not dumb enough to put my initials on a piece of paper bragging about how I took Dash."

"I know that. I had to ask."

Again, Dave smiled.

At that moment Nurse Carlton returned with the rest of the ice for Dave. I thanked her and said I needed to go to class.

I turned to look once more at Dave, who was now lying on his back with five ice packs spread out all over his body.

"Don't you worry, Dave. We're going to get you out of this mess."

"What am I supposed to do in the meantime?"

I smiled and said, "You just stay cool."

11:41 a.m.

CHAPTER 13

11:42 a.m.

"**W**here have you been all this time?" Jenny asked when I returned to class.

"I was in the office talking to Dave."

"Why is your wrist all red?"

"Oh, no reason. Let's talk about Dave," I suggested, trying to change the subject.

"Do you still think he's innocent?"

"Yes."

"Did you find out anything about what happened to Dash?" she inquired.

"Yes. Dave said he was in the Maze Room during the party. He told me he walked in there to get his backpack and saw you, Lori, and Jessica."

"Yeah, that's right," Jenny confirmed. "I walked in, and Lori and Jessica were already there. Did he say anything else?"

"Yes. After the three of you left, he said Mr. Young and Mr. Nelson came in, and Mr. Young told him to leave."

"So, what do you make of all this?"

"Well, by my count, that's five people who were at the scene of the crime near the time of the theft. That means we have five suspects."

Jenny shot me a look.

"I mean, we have four suspects."

"That's better," Jenny said.

I had been through this situation twice before, and I understood how much pain I could cause if I accused a close friend of a crime.

"I know you didn't do it, Jenny."

"Thanks. I appreciate that."

"That leaves four possible suspects," I said.

"Well, Chase, I think there's one person we can rule out right away."

"Who's that?"

"Mr. Nelson."

"Why do you think we can rule him out?"

"He's a *librarian*. Who would ever think that a librarian would steal something so important?" Jenny asked.

"Who would ever think that a principal would steal something so important?" I responded sharply.

"Good point," she said, remembering what happened with our former principal, Mr. Andrews. "Maybe we shouldn't rule Mr. Nelson out so quickly."

I smiled. "I've learned you shouldn't rule out anybody right away."

"So, who do you think is the most likely suspect?"

"Actually, I think there are two people."

"Which two?"

I then braced myself for the conversation I was about to have with Jenny. I needed to be very careful at this point because I wanted to get my point across, but I didn't want to upset her.

"I know we've been down this road before," I said softly, "and I don't want to make you mad."

"It's OK. I know you're just trying to solve the crime and find Dash. I won't get mad. I promise. Please tell me who you think did it."

"I think Lori is the obvious suspect."

"Why do you think it was her?" Jenny calmly asked.

Wow, she's handling this better than I imagined, I thought to myself.

"You know how much she wants the three of you to spend the summer together, either at the science camp or that other camp. I even heard her say earlier this morning that she really didn't care which camp it was. She'd be happy as long as you were together."

"Yeah, so?"

"So, if Lori took the hamster and framed Dave, he'd get kicked off the team. Then, if the hamster suddenly reappears later today, she gets put back on the team with you and Jessica."

"I guess that would be true," she replied. "No matter what I say, though, you're still going to investigate her, right?"

"Yes."

"Well then, let's move on to your second suspect," Jenny suggested.

"I think the thief could also be Mr. Young."

"Lori's father? Why?"

"When I saw him in the office earlier, he wasn't very helpful. Now he's the leader of the team. He should be doing everything possible to help me find Dash, but you should have heard how he was talking to me, giving me a deadline and using a rude tone. It almost seems like he wants Dave to be the guilty one so if we find Dash in time, Dave wouldn't get to go to the race, and his daughter would."

Then Jenny brought up a great point.

"Whoever did this needed to be alone in the Maze Room, at least for a minute, right?"

"I guess so."

"Assuming Dave is telling the truth, if Lori did it, then she would have had to be alone in there before Jessica walked in. If her dad did it, then he would have had to be in there after Mr. Nelson left."

"That's true," I replied, realizing once again how helpful Jenny could be in times like these. "Do you know if Lori and Jessica walked into the Maze Room together before you got there?"

"No. Do you know if Mr. Young and Mr. Nelson left the Maze Room together?"

"No," I said. "I need to go back to the office and talk to Dave again. Once I get more information, I'll have a better idea what our next steps are."

"Do you want me to go with you?"

"No, thanks. Lunch is starting in a second. I'll go, and I'll meet you at the benches in a few minutes."

"Do you think Ms. Fletcher will let you talk to Dave?"

"I sure hope so," I answered. "Otherwise, the cafeteria is going to run out of ice."

12:09 p.m.

CHAPTER 14

12:10 p.m.

Boy, those two are spending an awful lot of time together today, I thought to myself when I entered the office at lunchtime and saw Ms. Fletcher talking with Mr. Young. *I wonder what's up.*

The two adults were so engrossed in their conversation that they didn't notice I was right outside the principal's office.

Though I knew I wasn't supposed to eavesdrop, I couldn't help myself. This sounded important. I hid with my back against the side wall and pressed my ear up against it.

"You really think he's been acting strangely today?" Ms. Fletcher asked Mr. Young.

"Oh, yeah, very strange," Lori's father replied.

"Who are they talking about?" I whispered to myself.

"Is it something we should be worried about?" the principal asked.

"Oh, yes, very worried," Mr. Young said. "I mean, after all, he has a big job at Apple Valley. He is the school librarian."

"Mr. Nelson!" I said to myself. "They're talking about Mr. Nelson."

Just then, the two adults stood up to leave Ms. Fletcher's office, and I realized I needed to make a move. I walked forward and met them at the door.

"Chase, what are you doing back here?" Ms. Fletcher asked.

"I brought Dave his lunch. Where is he? I thought he'd be sitting out here by now."

"I'm afraid he's still in the nurse's office. He's pretty banged up," she said.

"Ouch, that's too bad," I said, feeling guilty about slamming so hard into Dave earlier.

"Leave his lunch with me," Mr. Young commanded. "I'll give it to him. You run along now."

"But, I just wanted to talk to him for a second."

"I said I'll give it to him," Mr. Young repeated, his tone becoming even stronger.

"But—"

"Chase," Ms. Fletcher interjected, "we don't need to have another talk about respecting authority, do we?"

"No, ma'am," I said, dropping my chin to my chest and handing Dave's lunch to Mr. Young.

I had been denied.

12:22 p.m.

CHAPTER 15

12:23 p.m.

Even though I was about ten minutes late getting to the benches, Jenny still hadn't arrived. I sat down and started eating. All of a sudden, I heard footsteps behind me.

It was Brock Fuller.

"Hey, Fan, what's going on?"

"Oh, hi, Brock," I replied, "I'm just eating my lunch."

"Where's Shovel?"

"He's in the office."

"Oh, yeah, where else would he be?" Brock teased. "Well, later."

After Brock left, I closed my eyes and enjoyed the first quiet moment I'd had all day.

Just then, Jenny, Jessica, and Lori came out of the girls' bathroom and joined me on the bench. Jenny sat next to me while the other two sat across from us.

As Jessica and Lori compared lunches, Jenny whispered to me, "Did you get to talk to Dave?"

"No," I whispered back.

"Why not?"

"Ms. Fletcher and Mr. Young wouldn't let me. And he was really mean to me."

Jenny looked across the table and seemed to be studying Lori.

The four of us ate quietly for a few minutes before Lori opened the conversation.

"I still can't believe what Dave Morrison did this morning. I hope he gets in big trouble!" she said.

"Yeah," Jessica added, "I hope he gets expelled. Ex-pelled."

"Yeah," Lori agreed, "that would serve him right."

"You know what?" I said, joining in. "If Dave did steal Dash, I hope he gets expelled, too. That's what he deserves."

Jenny almost choked on her sandwich when she heard my comment. She then looked over at me.

When the other girls weren't watching, I gave her a wink.

"Do you really feel that way, Chase?" Lori asked.

"Of course, I do."

I think Jenny was beginning to realize what I was doing. She knew that Lori and Jessica had no idea I'd been trying to defend Dave all morning, and I didn't want them to know that I now suspected Lori and her father. By pretending to blame Dave, I could keep the other girls in the dark.

"And if we find Dash and she wins the race today," Jenny said, playing along, "then all four of us should be on the science team and go to camp together."

"Absolutely," I said. "It would be great to go to summer camp with you girls."

"Yeah, great," Jessica said weakly, "really great. Excuse me, everybody, I need to use the restroom."

"But we went a few minutes ago," Jenny said.

"I…I know, but I need to go again," Jessica stammered, clutching her stomach and running off.

A short time later, the rest of us had finished eating.

"Let's go play tetherball, guys," Jenny suggested.

"Should we wait for Jessica?" asked Lori.

"No, she can meet us there," Jenny said. "Are you coming, Chase?"

"I can't," I answered. "I need to go do some business."

12:46 p.m.

CHAPTER 16

12:47 p.m.

I entered the boys' bathroom to do my business and immediately felt a big drop of water hit my right shoulder.

"Dude, what the heck is that?" I said to myself as I saw the wet spot on my shirt. Then I shook my head. "I must be spending too much time around Brock. I'm starting to talk like him."

A second later, it happened again. This time a larger drop of water hit me on the same shoulder.

I looked up, turned, and noticed the water was dripping from the air vent above the bathroom stall. When I was finished, I walked out and scanned the area. I didn't see any water dripping from the other vent across the room. Each vent was about two feet wide and two feet tall, and a metal piece with five vertical slits allowed heat to flow into the bathroom on cold days.

As I stepped to the sink to wash my hands, I heard a rattling sound. The metal cover piece, I observed, had some loose screws and was jiggling a little.

"I better tell Kenny about this the next time I see him," I whispered to myself. "That cover could fall off and hurt someone."

The rattling sound grew louder, and it looked as if the metal piece was going to hit the ground any minute. There wasn't time to find the school custodian. I was going to take care of this myself.

Now.

I climbed up on the toilet and decided to tighten all four of the screws. But when I started on the first one, the entire cover piece detached from the wall and fell into my hands.

"Wow, that sure came off easily," I said, surprised. "I'll just put this back."

As I tried to lift the cover piece back into position, I noticed how much empty space there was in the vent.

"I didn't know this much room was back here," I said to myself. "Why, you could fit a—"

And then it hit me!

A burst of energy filled my body, and I quickly worked to tighten all four screws. Right when the cover piece was secure, the bell rang, and I hustled back to class.

I knew where to find Dash.

12:55 p.m.

CHAPTER 17

12:56 p.m.

I returned to the room with a plan. Writing Workshop time was about to begin, and Mrs. Kennedy wanted all of us to open our writing notebooks and start brainstorming story ideas. She called them seeds. Next week, after we had collected a few seeds and tried them out to see which was our favorite, we would begin drafting our stories. Normally, I enjoyed this process very much.

Today, I had other things on my mind.

"Psst, Jenny," I whispered to my neighbor.

"Yeah, what's going on?"

"I have to go somewhere, and I need you to do me a favor."

"What is it?"

"If I'm not here in half an hour, ask Mrs. Kennedy to let you go to the office and say she needs me back in class."

"What? Why? Where are you going?"

"I don't have time to explain. Gotta go."

"Boy, he's exasperating!" she exclaimed as I left the table.

I went to Mrs. Kennedy's chair seeking permission to leave the room. Fortunately, she was busy meeting with another student and let me go without asking any questions. A few seconds later, I was out the door and heading down the hallway.

Though my mind was focused on the next step of my plan, I saw something out of the corner of my eye and came to a complete stop. Someone was running across the playground and heading to the gate next to the teachers' parking lot.

It was Stanley Nelson.

I wasn't sure if this was anything to worry about, but I did remember Mr. Young talking with Ms. Fletcher at lunch about how strangely Mr. Nelson had been acting today.

I decided to check it out.

Hiding behind a wall so the librarian wouldn't see me, I watched as Mr. Nelson got to his car that was parked on the street right outside the gate. I observed that all four windows were rolled down about three inches. Mr. Nelson opened the rear door on the driver's side of the car and appeared to be examining something in the backseat.

In the boys' bathroom at the end of lunch, I thought I'd figured out Dash's location. But now, after seeing Mr. Nelson behave so suspiciously, I wasn't 100% sure anymore. I didn't think the librarian had been acting *that* strangely today, but I did notice how uncomfortable he was with today's hamster race.

Mr. Nelson had made it very clear that he didn't like competition and wished everyone could be on the travel team. I even noticed the pained expression on the librarian's face when he saw how upset Lori was about not getting to go to this afternoon's event.

Could he have taken Dash to keep her out of the race so nobody else at Apple Valley would feel the disappointment of losing? I wondered. *And, could Dash be in the backseat of his car? Could the windows be rolled down so she could breathe?*

A minute later, Mr. Nelson shut the rear door and opened the front one. From behind the wall where I was hiding, I couldn't get a good view of what was happening. But when the librarian started walking back to the library, I was ready for him.

"Hi, Mr. Nelson, may I talk to you for a minute?" I asked, popping out from behind the wall.

Immediately, Mr. Nelson jumped back. "Oh, hi, Chase. Where did you come from?" He held his hand to his chest and tried to catch his breath.

"Oh, I was just walking down the hall. May I ask you a question?"

"Sure, what is it?"

"Why were you running to your car a minute ago?"

Mr. Nelson became very upset, and I could almost see steam coming out of his ears.

"You know, Chase, I get so mad thinking about it. I was putting more coins in the parking meter so I don't get a ticket."

"You were?" I said, caught off guard by his answer.

"Yes. Can you believe that I've worked here for two years, and I have to park on the street?"

"You do?"

"Yes. I had a spot in the teachers' lot, but a few weeks ago Ms. Fletcher gave it to Mr. Young."

"She did?"

"Yes. Can you imagine that? Kicking a teacher out of the teachers' parking lot so a parent can park there! It's outrageous!"

"Wow, that's rough, Mr. Nelson. And you have to put money in the parking meter every day?"

"Three times a day!" the librarian corrected.

I wasn't sure what to believe. If Mr. Nelson was telling the truth, his running across the playground now made sense. He very well could have been worried about his meter running out and getting a ticket. Also, since I was blocked for a minute, Mr. Nelson could simply have been putting coins in the parking meter during that time.

I believed Mr. Nelson's story, but I wasn't ready to let him off the hook.

"Mr. Nelson, are you looking forward to today's hamster race?"

"Honestly, Chase, I'm not."

"Why is that?"

"Well, you know how I feel about competition. I get very sad when young people have to lose. I wish everyone could get along, cooperate, and do things together, like read."

"Read?"

"Yes, and speaking of reading, yesterday I received a shipment of new books that I know you're all going to love. In fact, they're still in my car."

"Can I get a look at them?" I asked, wanting to see for myself what exactly was in the backseat.

"Well, why not? I'm not supposed to keep you from your learning, but this will only take a minute."

After a short walk across the playground, the two of us reached his car. Sure enough, three boxes of books filled the backseat.

"See, there they are," the librarian said, as if he were the proud father of these books. "Check out these little babies."

"Why do you keep your windows rolled down when the only things back here are books? Aren't you supposed to leave air just for *living* things?"

"To me, Chase, books are living things, and all living things need air to breathe, right? I sure don't want to hurt these little babies."

That sealed it. I realized that nobody who referred to books as "little babies" and left the windows down so they could breathe was ever going to steal a real living thing like a hamster.

"Thanks for showing me the books, Mr. Nelson. You're right. They look great." I liked the librarian. Sure, he was a little different, but he cared about kids and cared about reading. I respected that.

"No problem, Chase. Why don't you head back to class now."

"See you later," I said.

Mr. Nelson began walking toward the library. I went in a different direction.

I wasn't ready to head back to class yet.

1:06 p.m.

CHAPTER 18

1:07 p.m.

After checking to make sure the coast was clear, I made a run for it and safely arrived at the door of my next stop. Without a doubt, I had found myself in some frightening situations over the past few months.

In the hallway with Brock Fuller.

In the car with Coach Turner.

In the security room with Mr. Andrews.

In the gardening shed with the door locked.

Still, at this moment, nothing seemed scarier than the next place I was going to be.

In the girls' bathroom.

"Hello? Hello? Is anybody in here?" I called out before stepping inside.

There was no answer.

"OK, then," I said to myself nervously, "I guess I'm going in." I gathered my courage and took a few steps inside, my hands covering my eyes.

All of a sudden, I heard squeaking. The noise was faint at first, but then it grew louder. I recognized the sound immediately.

It was Dash running on her exercise wheel!

In the tiny, one-foot-by-one-foot cage where our team kept the hamster, we had also put a water cup, a toy, and a small exercise wheel.

That squeaky wheel was now music to my ears.

"I knew it! I knew it! I knew Dash would be in here," I said, becoming more comfortable in my new surroundings.

Just as I thought, two vents were built into the walls on opposite sides of the room, exactly as they had been in the boys' bathroom.

"Dash's cage must be behind the metal cover piece in one of the vents," I reasoned.

Because of the way the sound bounced off the tiles, I couldn't tell which vent contained Dash's cage, but I knew it had to be one of them.

"Now that I know she's in here," I said to myself, "I have just one more decision to make. Do I leave her here, or do I take her with me?"

Even though it might have seemed obvious that I should find Dash and grab her now, I quickly realized that locating the hamster was only one piece of the puzzle. I also had to prove that Dave didn't do it.

I put my head in my hand and thought for a while about this difficult decision. I concluded that the better choice was also the riskier one—to leave Dash behind and hope she was still there later in the day when I returned for her.

After all, I figured, if I carried Dash back to the library now, everyone would think that Dave told me where she was. And if they thought I was covering for Dave, then he'd still be kicked off the team. Also, if Dash were removed from her hiding place in the girls' bathroom, I knew it would be harder to prove who the real thief was.

With my mind made up, I walked to the door. Before leaving, I turned around to say one last thing to Dash.

"I'll be back for you in a little while, girl. You just keep rolling."

1:18 p.m.

CHAPTER 19

1:19 p.m.

I exited the girls' bathroom with my fingers crossed. I hoped with all my heart that Dash would remain safe up in the vent until I could carry out the next step of my plan. I also hoped that nobody would catch on to what I was doing. As I walked out the door, however, I saw a tall figure coming up the hallway towards me.

It was Patty Fletcher.

Oh, no! I thought to myself. *I can't let her find out that Dash is in the girls' bathroom. If the principal knew that, then she'd take the hamster out of the vent now, Dave would still get blamed, and I wouldn't have a chance to finish my plan. I have to stay calm.*

When Ms. Fletcher saw me standing by the door of the girls' bathroom, an angry expression appeared on her face, and she charged at me like a bull.

"This isn't going to be pretty," I mumbled, preparing for the worst.

"Chase, is that you?" the principal called out.

"Yes."

"What are you doing here?" she asked firmly. "I can't think of one good reason why you'd be standing outside this door."

"I...I was just using the restroom," I answered weakly.

"Chase, you know you're a boy, don't you?" she said sarcastically. "This is the *girls'* restroom. Surely, you know the difference."

I didn't like where this conversation was going. "Yes, of course, I do. I was—"

"You know you're not supposed to be here," she interrupted.

"I know, but—"

"I simply can't believe this," she once again interrupted. "After I've already spent valuable time today talking to you about your behavior, I find you hanging out outside the girls' restroom."

"Ms. Fletcher, I wasn't exactly hanging out."

"This is unacceptable!" she declared. "Apparently, you haven't learned your lesson."

"But I have," I said, trying to protest.

"I don't agree. I'm sending you to the office right now," she announced.

"Please, I can explain."

"I don't have time to listen to your excuses. I have someplace important that I need to be, and you're making me late."

"But—"

"Chase, I don't need to talk to you anymore about respecting authority, do I?"

"No, ma'am."

"Good. You go sit outside my office, and I'll be there as soon as I can."

"OK."

Ms. Fletcher then walked up the hallway while I headed in the other direction.

"Jenny better come get me soon," I said to myself. "Or else, I may be sitting in there for the rest of the day."

A few moments later, I arrived at the office, took a seat, and waited. One minute turned into five, and five minutes turned into ten.

There was still no sign of Jenny.

1:40 p.m.

CHAPTER 20

1:41 p.m.

"Chase, could you please settle down," said Mrs. Gonzales, the office manager. "You're tapping your feet and shaking your chair so loudly, it's distracting."

"I'm sorry," I replied. "I'm feeling very restless. I'm waiting for somebody, and she was supposed to be here by now."

"Well, Ms. Fletcher is a busy woman. I'm sure she'll be here as soon as she can."

Mrs. Gonzales didn't know that I wasn't talking about the principal. I was waiting for Jenny. I'd been gone from the classroom for more than thirty minutes, and she hadn't shown up yet.

Time was ticking away.

Where could she be? I thought, trying to settle down in my chair. I wished I could at least speak with Dave while I was waiting, but the iceman was still lying down in the nurse's office.

"I wonder if Jenny forgot," I whispered to myself. "Or, maybe Mrs. Kennedy wouldn't let her leave class."

Just as I was considering these possibilities, I heard footsteps coming through the entryway.

"Yes! It's Jenny!" I celebrated aloud.

But the footsteps didn't belong to Jenny Gordon.

They belonged to Patty Fletcher.

Oh, no, I thought, *she's going to call me into her office and talk to me some more about my behavior.*

Much to my surprise, however, the principal simply ignored me, walked into her office, and shut the door.

More waiting followed.

Finally, Jenny came through the entryway a moment later.

"Boy, am I glad to see you," I said.

She smiled and then knocked on the principal's door.

"Ms. Fletcher, may I ask you a quick question?"

"Oh, hi, Jenny. What can I do for you?"

"Mrs. Kennedy sent me down here to get Chase. We need him for a class activity. May I take him back to our room?"

The principal hesitated.

"Well, I'm not sure. Your friend is having a hard time following directions and respecting authority today."

"Please, Ms. Fletcher, my teacher said it's very important that I bring Chase back with me."

"OK, on one condition."

"What's that?" Jenny asked.

"Chase needs to apologize to me," the principal replied.

Hearing every word of this conversation, I wasn't happy about having to apologize for my behavior, but at this point, I was going to do whatever it took to get out of the office and continue with my plan.

"Ms. Fletcher, I'm sorry," I said. "I apologize for my behavior today."

"I accept your apology, but remember one thing," the principal said.

"What's that?"

"Don't ever disobey me again!"

With that, Jenny and I returned to class.

Mrs. Kennedy was waiting for me the second I walked through the door.

"Chase, what's going on? You've hardly spent any time in class today."

"I know, Mrs. Kennedy," I said. Then I paused. I knew my teacher was the one adult I could trust more than any other, so I pulled up a chair and looked her right in the eye. "It's... it's just that—"

"It's what, dear?" she asked softly.

"It's been another one of those days."

She immediately seemed to know what I was talking about.

"It's all right, Chase. I understand."

"You do?" I asked, relieved.

"Yes. Why don't you sit down and go back to your writing," she suggested.

"Actually, I'm afraid I can't do that," I said as gently as possible. Mrs. Kennedy was already being incredibly understanding, and I didn't want to push it.

"Whatever do you mean?"

"I know this might sound strange, but in a few minutes Jessica is going to ask to use the restroom. I'm going to need to follow her."

"What? Why?"

"I know I'm asking a lot, but I have to follow her."

"Is this about Dash?"

"Yes."

"Fine. I'll let you go."

I was so happy to hear this news, I once again reached out and gave my teacher a nice fist bump.

Sure enough, a few minutes later, Jessica approached the teacher's chair, clutching her stomach and bouncing up and down.

"Mrs. Kennedy, may I use the restroom? It's an emergency. A serious emergency."

"Go right ahead."

As soon as Jessica left, I looked up at my teacher. She looked back at me with a smile and nodded toward the door.

In a flash I was outside. Jessica Kingman was heading towards the girls' bathroom.

I was right behind her.

2:05 p.m.

CHAPTER 21

2:06 p.m.

Because of all the detective shows I liked to watch on television, I knew to keep a safe distance from Jessica Kingman on her way to the girls' bathroom on the other side of campus. Trailing too close might blow my cover. So, while Jessica walked straight for the door, I ducked behind walls, darted behind bushes, and hid behind drinking fountains. If Jessica discovered me before reaching her destination, she might ignore Dash completely and ruin my plan to catch her in the act.

My investigation would probably be all over.

Fortunately, I arrived at the girls' bathroom without being noticed. Jessica had already entered, and I waited right outside, ready to pounce.

"Hi, Dash. Hi, girl. I'm back. Did you miss me? I bet you missed me," she sang out.

That was all I needed to hear.

"Aha! So it was *you*!" I snapped, jumping out from my hiding place.

Jessica was stunned. She put her hand to her heart and gasped.

"Admit it," I said, now in full attack mode. "You took Dash and wrote that note to make it look like Dave did it. Shame on you."

"Chase, what are you doing here?" Jessica asked.

"I came to catch you taking Dash out of the vent. I know what you're up to. You're going to take Dash and put her back in the Maze Room. Then, when everyone arrives for the meetup, they'll be so happy to see her. They'll still blame Dave, and he'll get kicked off the team. Mr. Young will put Lori on the team, and if we win today, you and your friends will be able to go to camp together while Dave gets punished for no reason."

Jessica stood there quietly and listened to what I had to say. She took a deep breath and seemed to settle down a bit. Then, much to my surprise, she calmly said, "Chase, you're right. You're right."

"I am?"

"Yes. I give up. I'm tired of pretending. I admit it. I confess. I did put Dash in the vent. I was just about to get her now. She's been safe the whole time. I promise I kept her safe. I've checked on her a couple times, and I made sure her water cup was always full. Full of water."

Though I was deeply disappointed by Jessica's actions, I was impressed by her courage. I knew it wasn't easy to admit all this, and I was proud of her. "I'm really glad you told me all that, Jessica."

"Thanks. Thanks a lot."

"Doesn't it feel good to come clean and admit everything?"

"Yes, it does actually," she shared. Jessica then dropped her head down and put her hand in front of her face. It looked as if she had started to cry.

"It'll be OK, Jessica. I'll climb up and get Dash, and then we'll walk back to class together."

"OK," she said, all choked up.

I gave her a little smile.

"By the way, how did you know it was me?" she asked.

"I didn't at first. I thought Lori did it."

"Why her?"

"She had the strongest motive."

"Motive?"

"Yes. She had the most powerful reason to do it. She really wanted to go to camp with you and Jenny, but when she didn't make the team and when Dash looked so good in the exhibition this morning, it looked like going to camp together this summer wouldn't happen."

"What changed?" she asked.

"Then I realized you had the same motive. You also wanted to go to camp as a group."

"Yeah, but so did Jenny. Out of all three of us, when did you suspect it was me?"

"At lunch."

"What happened at lunch?"

"Two things. First, I thought it was strange that you went to the restroom after going with Jenny and Lori a few minutes earlier. I started wondering if there was another reason for doing that."

"What was the second thing?"

"The second thing was that when I went into the boys' restroom, I discovered how much space there was in the heating vent. There was more than enough room in there to fit Dash's cage. And when the cover piece came off so easily, I just put two and two together."

"What does that mean?"

"It means I figured out that you probably went to the restroom a couple times because you put Dash in there and wanted to check up on her."

"Boy, Chase, I've got to hand it to you. You're as smart as they say you are. Yes, sir. Smart as a whip."

I appreciated the compliment. "Now tell me, Jessica, which vent is Dash in?" I knew there were two, just like in the boys' room—one by the front door and the other near the back wall.

Still sobbing, she pointed to the vent farthest from the door. "I put him over the stall in the back of the restroom. In the back."

Then, I went in the last stall and climbed up on the toilet to reach the vent. When I turned away from Jessica to remove the cover piece, I felt something slam hard right behind me.

The next thing I knew, the door to the stall had been locked. Standing on the toilet, I turned around and saw Jessica take the cover off the vent on the other side of the bathroom and grab Dash.

With hamster in hand, she looked at me and said, "You may be smart, Chase, but not as smart as I am. No, sir. Not as smart as me."

"Wait!" I replied. "You can't leave me here!"

"So long, sucker."

In a flash I got down from the toilet and tried to open the stall door so I could run after her, but I couldn't do it. I tried again, this time pulling with all my might. It was no use. The door wouldn't budge.

Jessica was gone. The door was stuck.

I was trapped.

2:16 p.m.

CHAPTER 22

2:17 p.m.

I tried not to panic. With the meetup less than thirty minutes away, I immediately started searching for a way out of the bathroom stall. I attempted to climb over, slide under, and unwedge the door.

Nothing worked.

There was simply no way out. I sat on the toilet with my head in my hands trying to figure out my next move. Being trapped, I realized, wasn't my only problem. If Ms. Fletcher discovered me in the girls' bathroom, I knew I'd be in big trouble. I didn't even want to think about what might happen to me.

A moment later, I heard a young girl singing to herself as she entered the bathroom.

"To-ny Chest-nut knows I love you, To-ny knows, To-ny knows," she chanted.

Listening to her voice, I figured she must have been in kindergarten or first grade.

"Hello, is someone there?" I said, rising to my feet behind the stall door.

"Where is that voice coming from?" the startled girl replied as she looked around the room.

"Hi, I'm locked inside one of the stalls."

"Really?"

"Yes. What's your name?" I asked.

"Are you a boy?"

"Uh, yes," I said, a bit embarrassed.

"What are you doing in the girls' room?"

"Oh, it's OK. My name is Chase. Can you help me?"

"Hi, Race, my name is Cindy. I'm in kindergarten."

"No, Cindy, my name isn't *Race*. It's *Chase*."

"Oh, Race, did you know that one time I went to the beach with my mommy and daddy?"

"That sounds great, Cindy, but I really need your help."

"Race, I also went to the zoo once with my grandma and grandpa."

"That sounds fun, Cindy. It really does, but I need your help."

"Race, did you know they have animals at the zoo?"

"Yes, Cindy, I think I heard that somewhere. Can you help me? I'm stuck inside this stall."

"Well, I need to go now. Goodbye, Race," she said, not at all grasping the seriousness of my situation.

"Wait, you don't understand! I need your help!"

"Goodbye, Race."

With Cindy gone, I sat back down on toilet and started shaking my head in frustration.

More time passed.

More frustration.

Suddenly, I heard loud footsteps outside in the hallway.

"Please don't be Ms. Fletcher. Please don't be Ms. Fletcher," I repeated to myself with my fingers crossed.

As the steps grew closer, I could hear whistling.

"Phew! It's Kenny!" I said, relieved.

I decided to scream as loudly as I could to get the custodian's attention.

"KENNY! HEY, KENNY!"

"Is that you, Chase?" Kenny asked as he entered the girls' bathroom.

"Yes, I'm in the last stall."

"What are you doing in here?" the custodian said, trying to hide his laughter.

"I'm trapped in the stall. Please get me out of here," I said, a little embarrassed. I didn't find the situation nearly as funny as Kenny did.

"How did this happen?"

"It's a long story," I replied. "But the short answer to your question is that Jessica locked me in here."

"That nice girl did this to you?"

I had to bite down hard on my lip at that one.

"Yes, that nice girl did this to me."

"Well, let's get you out of here," Kenny said, approaching the door and attempting to open it.

He couldn't do it.

"Boy, this door is really stuck," the custodian said, struggling to force it open.

"What I don't get, Kenny, is how she could jam the door so tightly just by slamming it with her own strength."

"She didn't," he said as he finally managed to release me.

"She didn't?" I asked.

"No, check this out," Kenny said, extending his hand.

"What is it?"

"It's a piece of metal. Jessica slid it into the lock, and it completely jammed the whole thing."

"Whoa, that's pretty smart," I had to admit.

"Actually, it is," Kenny agreed.

"Well, thanks. I really appreciate your help."

"Are you sure you're OK? Do you want to stay and talk for a minute?"

"Thanks, but I can't."

"Why not?"

Then a feeling of total determination took hold of me, and I looked the custodian right in the eye.

"I have a thief to catch."

2:37 p.m.

CHAPTER 23

2:38 p.m.

I took a quick look at my watch on the way back to class and realized that everything with my plan was going to work out fine. The meetup hadn't started yet, and I'd still have plenty of time to tell everyone about Jessica's confession and clear Dave's name. I began to relax a little bit and took a few deep breaths.

Right outside my classroom door, though, I felt someone tap me on the shoulder.

It was Patty Fletcher.

Oh, no! I thought to myself. *Did she see me coming out of the girls' bathroom?*

"Hello, Chase."

"Uh, hi, Ms. Fletcher."

"I need to talk to you."

"Is something wrong?"

"No, not at all. I need you to do me an important favor."

"Now?"

"Yes, of course, *now*," she responded.

"What is it?" I asked, hoping it would be a quick favor.

"I need you to take four boxes of finger paint from the office to Mrs. Colby's kindergarten room."

Immediately, something seemed fishy about this request. *Is this really an important errand that has to be done now,* I began to wonder, *or is the principal simply trying to keep me away from the meetup?*

Whatever her reasons, I knew this would not be a quick favor. If I hustled, I might be able to finish by three o'clock. There was no way, though, I'd be able to get it done before the start of the meetup.

"Why me, Ms. Fletcher?" I asked, sensing that my plan to catch Jessica and clear Dave was coming apart at the seams.

"For one thing, I want you to do it because you did such a good job a few weeks ago when I asked you to do the same favor, and I need to choose someone I can trust. And for another," she said, growing angrier, "I want you to do it because I said so. I have talked to you all day about respecting authority, and this is your chance to show you know how to do that."

Ms. Fletcher then walked upstairs to the library in a huff.

I didn't know what to do.

Brock Fuller happened to be walking up the hallway during my conversation with the principal and was listening the entire time.

"Dude, what's up?"

"I don't know what to do," I admitted.

"What do you mean?"

"Ms. Fletcher asked me to move those boxes, but I need to go upstairs and help Dave. I can't do both things at the same time. If only there was—"

Then I got an idea.

"Hey, Brock," I said, "could you do something for me?"

"What?"

"Could you move the boxes for me?"

"Dude, didn't she ask you to do it?"

"Yes."

"And you want me to do it for you?"

"Yes."

"Well, I'm supposed to be heading back to class, but you did a lot for me a few weeks ago when we worked together to find the missing batting glove. Dude, I'll do it."

"Thanks, Brock. I appreciate it."

"No problem, dude. I'll take care of the boxes. You go help Shovel."

I smiled and bolted upstairs to the meetup. At the door I checked my watch.

I was a couple minutes late.

I made a grand entrance into the Maze Room. It wasn't quite a Ricky Dempsey entrance, but it was good.

As I had predicted, the girls were jumping up and down together in a circle celebrating when I stepped inside. A depressed Dave Morrison was sulking in a chair. In the middle of the room, Dash was in her cage running on the exercise wheel. Ms. Fletcher was finishing some paperwork in the far corner with her back to me. Mr. Young was standing right by the door. The one team member who was not in the room was Mr. Nelson. He was probably outside putting coins in the parking meter.

All of a sudden, everyone saw me standing tall at the door with my hands on my hips, and they stopped what they were doing.

The girls stopped celebrating and looked over at me.

Dave stopped sulking and looked over at me.

Dash stopped running on her wheel and looked over at me.

Ms. Fletcher stopped her paperwork and looked over at me.

With everyone watching me, I turned to Mr. Young and asked him a few questions.

"Is it true we found Dash?"

"Yes, we did," Mr. Young replied. "It happened a little while ago. We all walked in here for the meetup, and there she was. Imagine that!"

"Yes, imagine that," I repeated. "And you decided to put Lori on the team after kicking Dave off for stealing the hamster?"

"Yes, I did."

"Well, after hearing this news, I have three words for all of you about these decisions."

"What are they?" asked a confused Mr. Young.

"Not so fast."

2:48 p.m.

CHAPTER 24

2:49 p.m.

I had barely gotten the words out of my mouth when Patty Fletcher charged at me from across the room and stood right in my face.

"I told you earlier this morning never to disobey me again! I said the same thing to you after lunch! And what happened? I asked you to move four heavy boxes to Mrs. Colby's room, and there's no way you could have done that already!"

"The boxes are getting moved, Ms. Fletcher. I asked Brock to do it."

"I didn't ask *Brock* to do it. I asked *you* to do it. You better have a good reason for disobeying me now!"

"I think I do."

"What is it?"

"I'm just trying to stick up for Dave. I think everyone has been really unfair to him today. Everyone's ready to believe the worst about him and ready to believe he could have possibly written that ridiculous confession note. I have tried explaining it all to you and Mr. Young today, but I haven't been given the chance."

The principal didn't respond right away. She paused for a moment, and her expression changed.

"You know something, Chase? You're right. You have tried to talk with Mr. Young and me, and we never gave you a chance. Go ahead and explain. We're listening now."

"Thanks," I said. "A little while ago, I was in the girls' restroom, and—"

Everyone gasped.

"I know, I know, it sounds strange to me, too, but I had to do it. Anyway, when I was there, I caught Jessica, and I know she's the one who took Dash. She confessed everything to me. She admitted that she put Dash's cage in the vent and framed Dave so Lori would be put on the team. She even locked me in the stall, and Kenny had to come get me out."

"Why, Chase, I have absolutely no idea what you're talking about," Jessica replied with a straight face.

"You don't?" I fired back.

"No, I don't. It's obvious that Dave did it, and no matter what you say, Mr. Young made the right decision putting Lori on the team."

Seeing Jessica's true colors, I dropped my head to my chest and started shaking it. Any last bit of respect I had for her was now gone.

"It's too bad, Chase, that you can't prove one bit of what you said. You're usually better than that."

Rather than get upset by Jessica's comment, I simply smiled.

"Why are you so happy?" she asked.

I had come to this meeting prepared. I knew there was a chance Jessica wouldn't own up to everything, so I added one more part to my plan.

"I was hoping it wouldn't come to this," I said. "I was hoping that instead of denying it, Jessica, you would be honest about what you did and take responsibility for your actions."

"What are you talking about?" she said.

"When I made my first visit to the girls' restroom, I put an invisible powder all over Dash's cage."

Eyebrows rose throughout the room.

"After a certain period of time," I continued, "that powder leaves behind a stain on the hands of every person who has touched the cage since I left. In fact, we will find that stain on the hands of someone in this room VERY soon."

I then looked down at my watch and did some quick arithmetic.

"According to my calculations, that stain will appear on the thief's hands in 3, 2, 1…now."

Standing next to Dave, I held up my friend's hands, showing no stain.

The only person who looked down at her hands to check for a stain was Jessica Kingman.

"See," Jessica said, breathing a sigh of relief, "no stain."

"Of course there's not. I was only bluffing about the powder. I wanted to see if you would look down, and you did."

Jessica knew she had been outsmarted.

"There was no powder?" she asked in disbelief.

"No. I saw that on a TV show once. The officers used that trick to catch the bad guy who stole some important stuff."

"You mean the bad guy looked down at his hands the same way I did?" Jessica said, sniffling.

"Works every time," I said.

"Why did you do this, Jess?" Jenny asked softly.

"I just wanted us all to be together, but when *you*," she said, pausing for a moment and pointing angrily at Lori, "when you dropped the ball this morning, I had to bail you out by taking Dash and framing Dave. You let him get a higher score. You let him *beat* you. I wanted us all to go to camp together. Together! I even bought new clothes!"

After hearing Jessica's emotional outburst, I turned to the principal and said, "Ms. Fletcher, take her away."

The principal began walking Jessica out of the room.

Mr. Young turned to me and said, "There, are you happy now?"

"No, we need to do two more things," I replied.

Ms. Fletcher stopped walking so she could hear what I had to say.

"Oh, yeah? What are they?" Mr. Young asked.

I moved next to Dave. "First, we need to put Dave back on the team. Then everyone needs to give him a big apology. All he did today was study as hard as he ever has for a test, and then he did really well on it. All everyone else has done is expect the worst from him and give him a hard time, with no real proof that he did anything wrong. We treated him unfairly, and we need to make things right."

Dave had a huge smile on his face as he listened to me defend him.

Then, one by one, every member of the team came over, shook his hand, and apologized.

There was one person who owed Dave a bigger apology than anybody else, and she came through like a true professional.

Patty Fletcher.

"Dave, I'm sorry for how I treated you today. I'm especially sorry for the comment I made to you before the exhibition race this morning. It was wrong, and it was unfair. I should know better. Your behavior frustrates me sometimes, but I realize that doesn't give me the right to talk to you that way. You earned your spot on the team, and I wish you luck this afternoon."

"Thanks, Ms. Fletcher," Dave said.

"Dave, you're officially back on the team," Mr. Young announced.

"All right!" Dave and I said together.

Just then, Stanley Nelson ran into the room out of breath.

"Come on, everyone, let's get ourselves organized," he panted. "The bus is ready. It's time for us to go."

3:00 p.m.

Epilogue

Following in the footsteps of Amy Simmons, Jessica Kingman became the second student in the past month to be expelled from Apple Valley Elementary. Patty Fletcher had to take care of all the paperwork right away and couldn't come with us as we made the trip across town for the hamster race. She also had to wait with Jessica until her parents could pick her up and help gather her belongings. I found out later that Jessica sat in the office crying while the principal completed all the necessary forms.

With Jessica off the science team, Mr. Young had his daughter fill the open spot, and the group now consisted of Jenny, Dave, Lori, and me. While Lori was happy about joining the team, her father was downright giddy. Facing the prospect of leading a team that didn't include his daughter had made him grumpy and edgy all day.

No longer was that the case.

He had rediscovered that spring in his step and was as forceful and commanding as ever. As the race was set to begin, Mr. Young took charge. He called all the shots and acted as if Stanley Nelson wasn't even there. Officially, the librarian was the leader of the team. In reality, Mr. Young controlled everything.

Prior to the start of the race, I looked at Dash and wondered whether spending several hours in the bathroom vent would affect her. I was worried. It turned out that I didn't need to be.

She once again performed like a champion.

In fact, her time of 11.9 seconds was the fastest in the history of the contest. She beat Diamond, Daisy, Dixie, Debbie, Darlene, Disco, and eleven other tiny creatures to become the state's "Most A-Maze-ing Hamster."

After Dash was the first to reach the cheese at the end of the maze, my teammates and I exploded in cheer as we realized we would be heading to science camp together this summer, free of charge.

As we celebrated, I sensed someone approaching from behind.

It was Ricky Dempsey.

"Hey, Jack," Ricky said.

I wonder what he wants, I thought to myself.

"Good race, Ricky," I said, trying to steer the conversation in a positive direction.

"Ricky has one thing to say to you, Jack."

"My name isn't Jack, Ricky. It's Chase."

"Jack, Chase, whatever. Ricky has one thing to say to you."

"What's that?"

"Your hamster rocks," Ricky said, holding out his hand and smiling.

"Thanks, Ricky," I replied, as we shook firmly. "Yours is pretty great, too. Second place is really good."

"Thanks, Jack, I mean, Chase."

"It's too bad the second place team doesn't get to go with us this summer," I said. "It would be fun to go to camp with you."

"Well, Ricky's parents said they might pay to send Ricky there anyway, even if Ricky can't go for free."

"That would be awesome," I said.

Right at that moment, the person in charge of the event stepped to the microphone to begin the trophy presentation.

"I would like two members of the Apple Valley team to join me on stage," he announced.

Immediately, all four of us looked up at Mr. Young, hoping to get chosen to represent the school.

"Let's see," Mr. Young said, rubbing the bottom of his face as he thought it over. "Jenny, Lori, you girls go."

"Now wait one minute!" Stanley Nelson said, stepping forward. "I've had enough of this! I am the leader of this team, and I will decide!"

"What do you think you're doing?" Mr. Young asked.

"I'm taking charge. That's what I'm doing."

"Well, it's too late. I've already chosen Jenny and Lori to represent our team."

"That isn't fair," the librarian sharply responded. "We should pick the two students according to their test scores from this morning. After all, you were the one who said it's the fairest way to pick the team. And if it's the fairest way to pick the team, then it's the fairest way to choose our two representatives."

Mr. Young was speechless. He realized that Mr. Nelson had a point and decided to back down.

Jenny and I gave each other looks of surprise. We were happy that Mr. Nelson was finally standing up for himself.

Meanwhile, the event leader wasn't sure why it was taking so long for our team to send two kids to the stage.

"Uh, Apple Valley, we're waiting," he said, tapping his watch. "Could you please have your representatives join me on stage?"

"Jenny, Chase," Mr. Nelson said, "you two had the highest scores. Go ahead. Go up there."

Jenny and I both smiled. As the two of us were halfway to the stage, I stopped. Everyone in the crowd seemed to be wondering what was going on.

I turned around and walked back to the librarian. "Mr. Nelson, I've already had a couple chances lately to be in the spotlight. I'd like to let Dave go in my place."

"Are you sure?"

"I'm sure."

"Why, Chase, I think that's a very unselfish gesture."

I went over to Dave and told him he should be the one to walk with Jenny to the stage.

"Are you sure?" Dave asked.

"Yeah, I'm sure."

"Thanks, Chase."

"You deserve it," I replied.

Dave and Jenny accepted the trophy and brought it over to Mr. Nelson, Lori, and me.

Mr. Young was sulking in the corner.

Once everything quieted down, Mr. Nelson called the group together for one final conversation before we boarded the bus for the trip back to school.

"Did everyone have a good time this afternoon?" he asked.

Normally quiet, Dave spoke up first.

"You know," he said, "this was almost the worst day ever. I studied hard for the test, really hard. I did a good job, and I made the team. Then, even though I didn't do anything wrong, I got taken off the team. But because of my friend Chase, I can now say that this has been the best day of my life."

With that, the victorious Apple Valley team hopped on the bus and drove away.

Dave held the trophy and cradled it like a baby the entire way home.

About the Author

Steve Reifman is a National Board Certified Teacher, author, and speaker living in Santa Monica, California. *Chase Under Pressure* is the third installment in the award-winning Chase Manning Mystery Series. Be on the lookout for the next Chase Manning mystery coming soon.

Steve has also written several resource books for teachers and parents, including *Changing Kids' Lives One Quote at a Time*, *2-Minute Biographies for Kids*, and *22 Habits that Empower Students*. You can find teaching tips, blog posts, and other valuable resources and strategies for teaching the whole child at www.stevereifman.com. If you'd like to learn how to write a mystery of your own, read Steve's *The Ultimate Mystery Writing Guide for Kids* or check out "The Ultimate Mystery Writing Course for Kids" on udemy.com.